VIKING RAIDERS

First published in Great Britain by HarperCollins *Children's Books* in 2013
HarperCollins *Children's Books* is a division of HarperCollins*Publishers* Ltd,
77-85 Fulham Palace Road, Hammersmith, London, W6 8JB.

The HarperCollins website address is: www.harpercollins.co.uk

1

Text © Hothouse Fiction 2013
Illustrations © HarperCollins *Children's Books* 2013
Illustrations by Dynamo

ISBN 978-0-00-751402-1

Printed and bound in England by Clays Ltd, St Ives plc

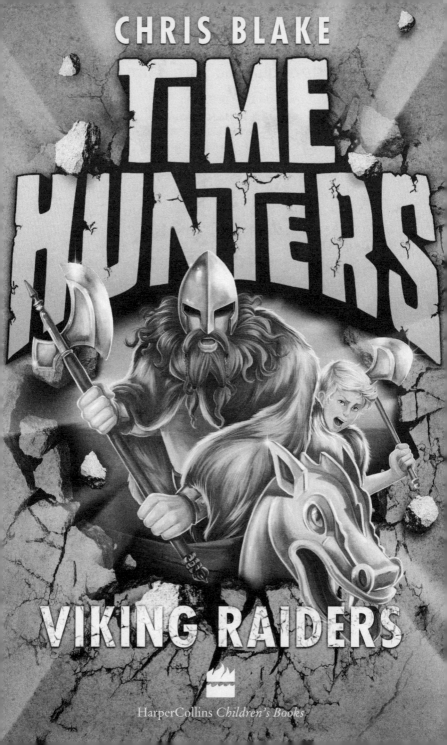

CHRIS BLAKE

TIME HUNTERS

VIKING RAIDERS

HarperCollins *Children's Books*

CONTENTS

With special thanks to
Marnie Stanton-Riches

PROLOGUE

Five thousand years ago

Princess Isis and her pet cat, Cleo, stood outside the towering carved gates to the Afterlife. It had been rotten luck to fall off a pyramid and die at only ten years of age, but Isis wasn't worried – the Afterlife was meant to be great. People were dying to go there, after all! Her mummy's wrappings were so uncomfortable she couldn't wait a second longer to get in, get her body back and wear normal clothes again.

"Oi, Aaanuuubis, Anubidooby!" Isis shouted impatiently. "When you're ready, you old dog!"

Cleo started to claw Isis's shoulder. Then she yowled, jumping from Isis's arms and cowering behind her legs.

"Calm down, fluffpot," Isis said, bending to stroke her pet. "He can't exactly woof me to death!" The princess laughed, but froze when she stood up. Now she understood what Cleo had been trying to tell her.

Looming up in front of her was the enormous jackal-headed god of the Underworld himself, Anubis. He was so tall that Isis's neck hurt to look up at him. He glared down his long snout at her with angry red eyes. There was nothing pet-like about him. Isis gulped.

"'WHEN YOU'RE READY, YOU OLD DOG?'" Anubis growled. "'ANUBIDOOBY?'"

Isis gave the god of the Underworld a winning smile and held out five shining amulets. She had been buried with them so she could give them to Anubis to gain entry to the Afterlife. There was a sixth amulet too – a gorgeous green one. But Isis had hidden it under her arm. Green *was* her favourite colour, and surely Anubis didn't need all six.

Except the god didn't seem to agree. His fur bristled in rage. "FIVE? Where is the sixth?" he demanded.

Isis shook her head. "I was only given five," she said innocently.

To her horror, Anubis grabbed the green amulet from its hiding place. "You little LIAR!" he bellowed.

Thunder started to rumble. The ground shook. Anubis snatched all six amulets and tossed them into the air. With a loud crack and a flash of lightning, they vanished.

"You hid them from me!" he boomed. "Now I have hidden them from you – in the most dangerous places throughout time."

Isis's bandaged shoulders drooped in despair. "So I c-c-can't come into the Afterlife then?"

"Not until you have found each and every

10

one. But first, you will have to get out of this…" Anubis clicked his fingers. A life-sized pottery statue of the goddess Isis, whom Isis was named after, appeared before him.

Isis felt herself being sucked into the statue, along with Cleo. "What are you doing to me?" she yelled.

"You can only escape if somebody breaks the statue," Anubis said. "So you'll have plenty of time to think about whether trying to trick the trickster god himself was a good idea!"

The walls of the statue closed around Isis, trapping her and Cleo inside. The sound of Anubis's evil laughter would be the last sound they would hear for a long, long time…

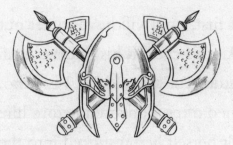

CHAPTER 1
SCARY MOVIE

"I want to go to the cinema too!" Isis said
to Tom over the breakfast table. "Please
take me with you!"

Her pet cat, Cleopatra, who was
sunbathing on the kitchen windowsill, mewed
in agreement.

Tom stared at the mummified princess
in disbelief. She was sitting on the edge
of the table, right next to Dad, and had

helped herself to a slice of his toast. Loose strands from her bandages drifted down into his porridge. Luckily, Isis was invisible to everyone except Tom. But even if Dad had been able to see or hear her, he was in a world of his own, reading *Archaeologist Weekly*.

No, he simply shovelled the porridge, now flavoured with five-thousand-year-old bits of Egyptian mummy, into his mouth.

"Mmm," Dad said. "Crunchy."

Tom suddenly lost his appetite. He jumped up from his chair and dropped his half-eaten cereal bowl in the sink with a clatter. Returning to the table, he took Isis by her crumbly arm and pulled her into the hall.

"Hey! I've not finished breakfast yet!" Isis grumbled.

"You don't need to eat breakfast – you're dead!" Tom said, letting go of Isis's bandaged arm. "And you can't come to the cinema with me because I know what you're like – you'll mess about and distract me."

Ever since he'd accidentally smashed a statue in his dad's museum, setting the Ancient Egyptian princess free, Tom had been stuck with Isis and her pet cat. And he'd continue being stuck with her until they found the six amulets that Anubus, the god of the Underworld, had scattered throughout the most dangerous times in history. So far they'd found two, but there were four more to collect.

"If you weren't such a troublemaker, we wouldn't be in this mess," Tom added, reminding Isis that their task was her punishment for cheekily trying to steal one of the amulets from Anubis.

"You've never had so much fun in your life!" Isis scoffed. "All these adventures! Since you met me, you've trained as a gladiator in Ancient Rome *and* met King Arthur! What do you offer me in return? Chess? History books? A GAME OF FOOTBALL?!" She started to make snoring noises.

"You're only saying that because you're rubbish at football," Tom said. He glanced into the kitchen and saw that Mum was busy wiping the worktops and Dad had his nose in his magazine.

Isis waggled her foot at him. "It's not easy kicking a ball when you're wrapped in bandages."

Tom breathed out heavily in frustration. "Do you even know what a cinema is?" he asked.

Isis shook her head sheepishly.

Tom explained that it was a place where stories were told along with moving pictures. "Everything on the screen is about ten times its normal size and the best bit is that it's really, *really* loud," he finished.

"Oh, I love stories," Isis said, clapping her hands in glee. "The priests in Egypt wrote the most amazing ones, with beautiful pictures

16

on papyrus scrolls. They used to read them to me when I was little. Sometimes, because I was so beautiful…"

Tom spluttered, but Isis ignored him.

"…they wrote me into the stories too!"

Tom hesitated. If he took Isis to the cinema, at least she wouldn't be able to cause mischief at home. He sighed. "All right, then. You can come with me."

Isis shuffled stiffly over to the front door and called out to Cleo. "Come on, Fluffpot! We're going to the cinema!"

Inside the cinema, the screen flickered brightly as the characters in the film blew up an old building containing fireworks. *Kaboom!* Rockets fizzed up into the night sky before exploding in a shower of colourful sparks.

As Isis cowered behind a row of seats Cleo yowled and clambered on to Tom's lap.

"Take cover, Fluffpot!" Isis cried to her cat. "The world is ending!"

Tom chuckled. "It's OK, you know," he said, reaching into a giant tub of popcorn. He put a fistful of the sticky kernels into

his mouth. "It's not real. The pictures can't hurt you."

Isis held her hands over where her ears would be. "What about the noise?" The explosions *were* quite loud.

"You'll get used to it," Tom told her.

"Are they gods?" Isis asked, pointing to the characters on the screen.

"They're just actors," Tom explained. He thrust his tub of popcorn towards Isis. "Here, try some of this. And be quiet because you're ruining the film for me."

Isis sat back on her seat nervously. She plunged a hand into the tub and stuffed some popcorn through a hole in the bandages that covered her face. "Mmm, this tastes great," she said, jaws creaking as she chomped away.

"Leave some for me!" Tom said.

Somebody's dad in the row behind leaned forward and tapped Tom on the shoulder.

"Hey! Keep it down, son. I didn't pay to listen to you talking to yourself for an hour."

Tom slumped down in his seat. He was glad that, in the dark of the cinema, nobody could see his cheeks glow.

Isis giggled and kept hold of the popcorn tub. "You heard the man," she said. "Stop ruining the film for everyone!"

Tom looked longingly at his popcorn.

"Can I have some, please?" he whispered, checking that the man behind wasn't listening.

Isis ignored him. The yellowy bandages on her face glowed white as she stared up at the flickering light of the screen. Isis started to laugh as the hero of the film said something funny.

Tom could tell she was utterly absorbed in the thrilling story. "Isis!" he hissed, giving her a good poke with his elbow.

"Shh!" she hissed. "This is a good bit."

Tom's stomach growled. "I bought that popcorn for me. Give it back, will you?"

He was just about to snatch the tub out

of her hands when their row of seats started to rumble and shake. Tom looked up at the film. Was it part of the action? Were the special effects really that convincing?

"Look!" Isis suddenly yelped. "Anubis!"

There, looming above, staring down at them through angry red eyes, was the Egyptian god of the Underworld himself.

"Enjoying the show?" Anubis boomed.

His voice bounced round the cinema. He stood with his fist on his hip, baring his sharp teeth and twitching the pointy ears on top of his jackal's head.

Tom gulped. It was as though Anubis had stepped right out of the screen. But everyone else in the cinema was still laughing and saying 'ooh' and 'aah', as though they could only see the film they had come to watch.

22

"Why did you have to turn up now?" Isis said hotly, throwing a handful of popcorn in Anubis's direction. "Get out of the way! You're blocking my view."

Several people looked round and tutted loudly, as the popcorn rained down on them.

Anubis growled. "You know why I'm here, you cheeky girl," he boomed, making the curtains at the side of the giant screen flap. "It's time for your next quest."

"Not yet. I want to see how the story ends!" Isis shouted.

The ground started to shake violently. Tom was sure their entire row of seats had started to edge forward.

"You will do as I say, Isis Amun-Ra, or you will never enter the Afterlife," Anubis roared. "You are leaving to find your next amulet RIGHT NOW!!"

CHAPTER 2
ERIK THE RED

The three travellers hurtled through the tunnels of time, twisting and turning through the ages, as though they were on the scariest roller coaster in the world. They shot out of the end and flew through the air. One by one, they landed on the ground with a *thunk, thunk, flump.*

Tom was shaking so hard from the cold that he felt his chattering teeth might fall out.

"I'm f-freezing," he said. "Where on earth are we?"

Standing up and stretching, he looked about. They had landed on a riverbank that was covered with frost. Alongside them, a wide river flowed fast. Its choppy waters glittered in the winter sunshine.

"I d-don't know," Isis said, blowing on her hands. "But I th-think my f-fingers might f-fall off."

Tom glanced over at Isis. Apart from the sweeps of black kohl round her eyes and the beaded black plaits that made her look unmistakeably like an Ancient Egyptian princess, she was back to being a normal ten-year-old girl again. And Cleo was back to being a cat, covered in stripy fur.

Tom peered down at himself. "We're wearing trousers and tunics, like we did in King Arthur's time," he said. "But these cloaks are made from animal skins." He pulled his heavy, furry cloak round him more tightly to keep out the cold. "And this doesn't look like England."

To their left, Tom spied a dense forest of fir trees. It stretched right down to the river in a dark line. A big, brown moose with enormous antlers emerged from the forest and walked down to the water on its long legs.

Isis pointed to a ship that was moored just beyond where the moose was drinking. "What kind of a boat is that?" she asked.

Tom frowned. The vessel seemed familiar. It was very long and quite narrow. In the middle was a single, thick mast to which was attached a giant, square sail. Oars stuck out on both sides, like legs on a giant centipede. At the back of the ship was a curly tail. But at the front...

"Look at that!" Tom said to Isis. "See the dragon's head carved at the front of the ship? I recognise that style from the Viking room in Dad's museum. It's a longship."

"That's great, but where and when are we, Professor Smartypants?" Isis asked, wrapping a shivering Cleo under her cloak.

Tom beamed. "Moose. Pine forests. Freezing weather! I think we're in Scandinavia," he said. "We've landed in the time of the Vikings." As he rubbed his hands together to warm them up, he caught sight of a pile of weapons and armour in the longship. The axes and swords glinted at him dangerously.

"What are Vikings?" Isis asked, jogging on the spot, her frozen breath looking like puffs of smoke.

Tom thought back to everything he'd read about the Vikings in his encyclopedia. "Vikings were warriors that were brilliant at sailing. They conquered the sea in those amazing longships. The men were called

29

things like Ulf and Olaf and Magnus." He decided not to mention the part about Vikings being murderous, axe-wielding giants, who went on the rampage in search of gold.

Isis tutted. "I've never heard such silly names in my life. Ulf! It sounds like a small, barking dog."

"I think it means 'wolf'," Tom said.

"Never mind. Anyway, we've got to find the amulet for the big old wolf himself," Isis said. "Come on. Let's see if my magic ring will tell us where Anubis has hidden it."

Isis wore a gold scarab-shaped ring with an image of a goddess sitting on a chair. The goddess, also called Isis, was the protector of children and the dead. Isis had worn the ring when she was alive, and had even been buried in it. It had helped them out on their quests before.

"Where is my amulet, oh, beautiful and clever goddess?" Isis asked the ring now.

Silvery letters wafted up out of the scarab, into the air. They arranged themselves in sentences, which Tom read aloud.

"Fly abroad, across stormy seas
On a dragon's back, long and thin.
Fighting, looting, as you please
'Tis treasure you need to win.
If Vikings die, they are not pained,
Their souls for Valhalla yearn!
When flaming arrow on boat is trained
Be sure that jewel won't burn."

Tom stuck his tongue in his cheek and frowned. "Right," he said to Isis. "Maybe the dragon's back means the longship." He pointed over to the boat's carved front.

Isis nodded and stroked a purring Cleo. "Yes. It seems pretty obvious that the riddle is talking about a journey over the sea."

"Perhaps we'll be going somewhere in that boat," Tom suggested.

Just as he opened his mouth to ask Isis if she knew what Valhalla was, they heard shouting and loud voices coming their way.

Tom looked round and spotted a group of tall, terrifying men. They wore helmets and fur cloaks. At their sides, they carried the longest broadswords he had ever seen. They were running, like a herd of angry moose, down to the longship. The only obstacle that stood between them and their vessel... were Tom, Isis and Cleo.

"Are those the Vikings you were talking about?" Isis asked quietly.

"Yes," Tom said, gulping. "I'm afraid so. They tried to look as fearsome as possible in the hope that their enemies would keel over with fear just at the sight of them."

"Well, that little trick won't work on me," Isis said. But Tom could tell from the quiver in her voice that she didn't feel as brave as she was pretending to be.

Cleo yowled when she saw the strangers and darted into the folds of Isis's cloak.

At the head of the group, Tom noticed a Viking who was as tall and broad as a door – a hulking, muscle-bound man compared to the others. Bright-red hair hung down his back in wild, matted clumps. His bearded, ruddy face was covered in freckles. In his huge hand he swung a gleaming axe.

"Do you think that axe is meant for us?" Isis asked.

The red-headed giant thundered towards them. His steely gaze was fixed on Tom.

"We're about to find out," Tom said, trembling like a jelly. "Please don't kill us!" he shouted, holding his hands above his head in surrender, as the stranger came to a stop and loomed over him. Hardly daring to look into the Viking's fearsome face, Tom stared at the man's boots instead. He had the most enormous feet.

Tom hoped the Viking had understood his plea for mercy. Everywhere else that Anubis had sent them, he and Isis had magically been understood. He just had to hope that his English words had come out in Old Norse.

Beside Tom, Isis skipped backwards and forward. Her fists were balled, but next to the huge Viking, she looked like a chick trying to pick a fight with a cockerel. "Come on, then, you big red hairball!" she shouted up at him. "You don't mess with a princess!"

Cleo hissed and swiped a claw at the Viking. The little cat's stripy fur was standing on end. Tom admired his friends' courage.

"I am Erik the Red!" the man said in a voice so deep it seemed to come from his toes. He grabbed Isis by her cloak and held her up so that her fists punched helplessly at thin air. "And I'm going to knock your brains out for skulking about near my boat."

CHAPTER 3
JOINING THE CREW

"Please let her go, sir, she's only a little girl!" Tom pleaded, desperate for Erik to release Isis.

"Little girl?" Isis shrieked, outraged. "There is nothing little about me. I am royal – and I fight better than you ever will."

Erik burst out laughing and dropped Isis back to the ground in a heap of plaits and furry cloak. Cleo rubbed up against her, checking that she was all right.

"She's a feisty one, isn't she?" Erik said to Tom. "Where did you find her?"

"You wouldn't believe me if I told you," Tom said, laughing nervously. He decided to draw Erik's attention away from Isis, in case she annoyed him again. "So where are you and your men off to?"

Erik set his helmet straight on his head. As he did so, Tom caught a whiff of sweat and damp.

"We're about to go on a little expedition," Erik said. "There's nothing like a bracing ocean voyage to blow away the cobwebs."

Tom looked at the dragon at the helm of Erik's longship and remembered the words of the riddle. "Setting sail on your *long and thin* boat, are you?" Tom said loudly, trying to attract Isis's attention.

But Isis was busy trying to pull Erik's red beard.

"Sailing *across stormy seas*, eh?!" Tom shouted.

Isis finally turned to Tom and winked. "Can we come too?" she asked Erik, innocently.

Erik's fiery eyebrows bunched together in a terrifying scowl. "Children on a Viking raid? Are you trying to insult me?" he boomed. "This is a looting party, you know. Do you have any idea what me and my men will be doing?"

Tom pursed his lips and swallowed hard. "Er, setting fire to people's houses? Stealing? That kind of thing."

Erik grinned and slapped Tom hard on the back. "Precisely, lad! That's no pastime for a youngster like you. You'd only get in the way."

Tom felt their chance slipping away... if he didn't hurry up and convince Erik to let them come, they'd never get the amulet and he'd be stuck in freezing Scandinavia forever.

"We're brilliant fighters, aren't we, Isis?" he said.

Isis nodded. "Yes! Sword fighting with knights. Net fighting with gladiators. You name it, we've done it." She mimed shooting an arrow from a bow.

"*I've* been specially trained in archery by the captain of my father's Royal Guards."

Erik took off his helmet and started to scratch his scalp. His lips twitched, as if he was trying hard not to smile. "Tell you what," he said. "Prove to me you can fight, and I might let you come with us." He put his fingers in his mouth and gave a piercing wolf whistle. "Ho! Bjørn," he shouted to a blond-haired warrior, who was loading a sack on to the longship. "Throw us over some armour and an axe or two. These youngsters want to come with us!"

With the crew of the longship gathered round to watch, Erik rammed a helmet each on to Tom's and Isis's heads. Tom's was far too big and fell over his eyes.

"Why don't these helmets have horns?" he asked, pushing it back up. *Vikings in films*

42

and cartoons always wore horned helmets, Tom thought.

Erik looked down at him and frowned. "Horns? Don't be so stupid, boy! If we had horns on our helmets, the enemy would be able to grab them and just wrench them off our heads. You don't give your enemy helpful handles, son. What a funny idea!"

He gave them axes that were so sharp and lethal-looking that Tom wondered if he'd make it on to the boat with all his arms and legs.

"Now, if you're going to chop each others' heads off, be sure you don't dent the helmets!" Erik chuckled.

Finally, he passed them each a round shield that was made from wood and covered in iron rivets.

"Right." He clapped his hands. "Get on

43

with it then. We need to set sail soon."

The Viking crew stamped their feet on the ground. "FIGHT! FIGHT! FIGHT!" they chanted.

Realising they had no choice if they were to find the amulet, Tom and Isis shrieked at the tops of their voices, rounding on each other with a *clang!* of metal as their axes met.

Isis backed away, wrenching her axe apart from Tom's. Tom waved his above his head, in a bid to look as menacing as possible.

"Huh! Anyone can do that!" Isis said, lifting her weapon into the air and swinging it round.

Cleo skipped between Tom and Isis, mewing loudly and chasing her tail.

But Tom could tell Isis was struggling with the weight of the axe, as her arm faltered. Suddenly, Cleo darted into her path, sending Isis off balance. Seizing the opportunity, Tom knocked her helmet clean off her head with the flat of his axe's blades.

"AAARRRGGGHHHHH!" he cried and split the helmet on the ground clean in two with his axe.

The watching crew exploded into deafening applause.

"Thor's hammer, give me strength! I thought I said be careful with the helmets!" Erik cursed. Chuckling, he added, "But I suppose that was a pretty impressive show."

"So we can come?" Tom asked hopefully.

Erik looked down at Tom and shook his head. "No, I'm afraid it's just too dangerous."

"Look, Mr Red, we're kind of desperate," Isis said, talking quickly. "There's an angry Egyptian god with a face like a dog and breath to match, who wants us to find a hidden amulet. If we can't go with you, we won't be able to find it and I'll never get into the Afterlife." She finally stopped to catch her breath.

Erik stared at her. Then he burst into laughter. "You spin a good yarn, little girl!" he said. "Go on then. Get on board before I change my mind. At least you two will liven up the long journey."

Isis grinned at Tom. "Where are we going?" she asked Erik.

Erik gazed out across the horizon. He pointed his finger west, across the sea. "To England, of course! The land of green fields, churches stuffed with gold, and home to a load of wimpy peasants." Then he punched his palm with a fist as big as a bowling ball. "We're going to grind them into flour for our bread!"

Erik turned and marched to the longship, his red hair and animal-skin cloak flapping in the wind.

Isis grabbed Tom's arm. "Why can't we go somewhere nice and warm?" she moaned. "This is the second time we've ended up going to that cold mud puddle!"

Tom shook her hand away. "Hey! That's my home you're talking about. I can't wait to see England through a Viking's eyes! This will be so cool."

Then Tom remembered what he'd read about how the Vikings had battled their way down the length of the country, murdering anything that breathed and destroying any town that stood in their path. He gulped, but it wasn't as if they had a choice. The riddle said they needed to board the longship if they wanted to find the amulet. "Come on," he said. "Our adventure begins here."

Erik introduced his men as the children stepped into the boat. "Bjørn the Bone-crusher!" Erik shouted. "Say hello to my new crew members."

Bjørn bowed to the three of them. "Be healthy! May your jug be always full of mead," he said in greeting. He tugged at his blond plaits and his stern face cracked into a smile.

Erik moved on to the next man. Tom's neck was beginning to ache from looking up at the tall men. It was the same routine with each one.

"Grisly Gunnar!" Erik bellowed.

Grisly Gunnar slammed down a fist on to Tom's shoulder. "Be healthy!" he boomed.

"May your sword be always red with the blood of the English."

"Er... thanks," Tom said, hoping that Grisly Gunnar never found out that he was English.

Just as Erik was about to go through the same routine with yet another man, Isis clapped her hands together like an impatient school teacher. "Hello, long-haired giants," she shouted at the top of her voice. "I'm Isis, he's called Tom, and this is my cat, Cleo. Nice to meet you. And yes, let's all be healthy! But can we just get on the boat and go now?"

CHAPTER 4
SETTING SAIL

On board the longship, benches ran from one side of the hull to another. The vessel rocked unsteadily as the bulky Vikings sat down. Tom tripped over their long legs as he and Isis looked for seats. The Vikings were all squashed together and there didn't seem to be any spaces left.

"Oh, great! Where are *we* going to sit?" Isis said.

"Come over here," a young man said, patting the tiniest of spaces at his side.

The man was taller than Tom and lankier than the other Vikings. He had white-blond hair that, like the others, he wore in long, fat plaits. His blue eyes were a little close together, but he looked friendly enough.

Tom and Isis squeezed on to the bench next to him.

"Be healthy! I'm Magnus," the young Viking said, offering Tom his hand.

Tom's fingers were almost crushed by Magnus's iron grip. He forced a smile through the pain. "Nice to meet—"

"And I'm Geir." A rich, rumbling voice interrupted Tom. He turned to his left and found himself looking into the lined face of a grey-haired man. He was much older than the other crew members.

"If you get seasick, be sure you don't do it on me," Geir said. His deep-set eyes sparkled playfully. "I'm wearing my best beaver skins."

Isis leaned forward and grinned at Geir. "If he *does* get seasick, I'm definitely pushing him in your direction." She stroked Cleo, who was sitting on her lap. "I'm wearing my best cat."

There was a *splash!* and a *clunk!* as Erik hauled the anchor over the side of the boat.

"Take up your oars!" he cried.

The men who were seated along the gunwale grabbed the long oars and started to rock back and forth in perfect time with one another. "Heave! Heave! Heave!" they chanted.

Creaking, the longship pulled away from the riverbank, and they sailed downstream towards the open sea.

"So, Magnus," Tom began, feeling like he ought to strike up some chit-chat with the stranger whose knee he was practically sitting on. "Are you excited to be on this voyage?"

Magnus beamed. "I certainly am. I'm as excited as a wolf howling at the moon."

"That excited, eh?" Isis asked.

"I can't wait to get to England," Magnus said. His smile drooped and his face sagged, as though the happiness had leaked out of him. "I can't stay at home, you see. My oldest brother, Arne, inherited all our family land. He and I don't get on, and he told me I would have to work as his servant. There's no way I'm going to do that!"

Tom frowned. "Are you really going to make enough money out of this expedition to live on?"

Magnus's eyes suddenly grew wide. His mouth curled back up into a smile.

"Why, yes! We're going looting, aren't we, lads?" he cried, punching the air. "To England! Where the streets are paved with gold. And the paths will run red with blood. HOORAH!"

The men sitting nearby all joined in, nodding their heads ferociously.

"OK!" Tom said, punching the air with what he hoped passed for enthusiasm. He didn't like the thought of hurting anyone. But he couldn't risk the Vikings finding that out, or that he was English.

With hardly any wind, and the water as smooth as glass, the longship cut through the river with barely a ripple. But Cleo had started to scratch and whine on Isis's lap.

"What's wrong, Fluffpot?" Isis asked.

Cleo spat.

"Oh! I know what's the matter with her," Isis said, clasping her hand to her head. "She absolutely hates water."

Suddenly, Cleo shot along the length of the ship and scampered up to the very top of the mast. "MEOOOOW!" She clung on to the wooden pole, trembling and meowing.

"Poor thing," Isis said. "She sounds so frightened. Come back down, kitty!"

Erik started to chuckle. He stroked his bushy red beard and erupted into a gale of hearty laughter.

"Looks like we've got ourselves a new look out, lads!" he said, pointing to Cleo.

The river grew wider and wider. Waves started to lap against the longship, making it rock from side to side. Soon, the waves grew taller, and crashed against the boat's hull.

"We're on the open sea, boys!" Erik shouted. He stood with his thick tree-trunk legs planted wide apart. Tom marvelled at his balance.

"Now, brace yourselves!" Erik continued "It's going to be a long journey. It will probably be dangerous too. But that doesn't matter, because we Vikings were born to sail, weren't we, lads?"

The men started to whistle and clap.

"Kings of the sea!" Magnus shouted.

Erik wagged his finger at him. "That's right! And don't forget, once we get to

England, all the gold and jewels and furs are ours for the taking. Enough for all of us!" He clasped his hand into a large, greedy-looking fist.

The longship's crew exploded into deafening whoops.

Geir stood up and waved his helmet in the air. "Those English can't fight," he shouted in his hoarse voice. "They're a bunch of WEEDS!"

Isis started to chuckle.

Tom poked her in the arm. "I managed to defeat you!" he whispered.

"And we will pluck those weeds!" Erik bellowed. He grabbed hold of one of the men's plaits and yanked it upwards, as if to demonstrate his weeding skills. Amazingly, the man didn't even flinch! "All we have to do is step ashore—"

"And grab the lot!" Bjørn cried, jumping up and down with such vigour that he tripped and crashed headlong into the row of men in front.

As the longship headed further out to sea, an icy wind battered the crew.

Tom pulled his fur cloak tightly round him, snuggling into its warmth. "I'm glad we've got these," he said.

Isis's teeth chattered. "H-h-how do you n-n-northern n-nincompoops m-manage in this terrible weather?"

Tom grinned. "We're made of strong stuff. Not like you softies from the south."

"V-v-very f-funny."

Night fell and the stars twinkled in the black sky. Four of the Vikings pulled a leather canopy across the top of the boat. Tom looked up, feeling sad he could no longer see the glow of the moon.

The crew lay on the floor of the longship to sleep, huddled together for warmth and smelling of fish – and worse.

"Get your feet out of my face!" Isis complained.

"My feet aren't anywhere near your face," Tom said.

"Then whose feet are they?"

"Mine!" came a gruff voice.

Isis wriggled like an angry eel. "Ugh! I'm so uncomfortable. I just want to stretch out."

"Well, you can't," Tom said.

Somebody wafted a salted fish in his face. It smelled of rotting socks.

"Want some more herring?" Magnus offered. "Or Geir's got some salted moose, if you fancy that."

"NO!" said Tom and Isis together. Though Cleo, who had caught a whiff of the fish, came down from the mast and was soon happily purring as she gobbled it up.

"I wish we'd never come here," Isis said.

Tom wiped his freezing nose on her cloak and whispered in the dark, "Anubis warned us that this would be our hardest mission yet. Anyway, it's not like we had any choice in the matter." Trying to cheer his friend up, he added, "Don't worry. I'm sure we'll find the amulet soon."

"How? We don't even know where to look," moaned Isis.

"The riddle mentioned fighting and looting. I'm sure we'll be doing plenty of that when we get to England."

"If we survive the journey, that is," grumbled Isis.

As dawn broke, Tom felt the ship rock violently up and down. It was like being on a roller coaster of enormous waves. The wind blew so hard that the canopy was almost ripped off the boat. Even the Viking crew looked worried, as they struggled to keep the longship under control.

"Do you think Anubis is making the wind?" Isis called to Tom.

"No!" he yelled back, clutching at Isis's cloak. "We're just in the middle of a billion-force gale!"

CHAPTER 5
STORM AT SEA

"I'm not feeling very well!" Tom groaned, clutching his stomach.

The longship rose up to the crest of a giant wave, then plunged back down the mountain of water. Tom felt his stomach float up to the top of his ribcage. It was like a never-ending fairground ride that wasn't fun any more.

Isis clung on to the bench with white

knuckles. "Just don't speak to me. At all."
Her face was as grey as the stormy clouds.
"I'm f-feeling a b-b-bit queasy." She clapped
a hand over her mouth.

Tom looked at the front of the ship and
saw Erik, standing tall, peering all about him.
He wrapped
his huge arms
round the
carved
dragon's neck
and ducked
low over the
water. Then he
pulled out a long
shred of cloth
and held it
high in the air,
flapping wildly.

"What's he doing?" Tom shouted to
Magnus over the deafening blast of wind.

Magnus, who was still pink-cheeked and
smiling, explained. "He is checking which
direction the wind is blowing in, to make
sure we're still travelling towards England.
In a gale like this, it's easy to get blown
off course."

"But what's that lump in his hand?"

Magnus chuckled. "Don't you know
anything about sailing, little fellow?"

The last boat Tom had been on was the
pedalo his mum and dad had hired when
they were on holiday in Spain. Vikings
were supposed to know about sailing, and
Tom was supposed to be a Viking. Thinking
quickly, he decided to bluff.

"Ha ha! Of course I do! I just couldn't see
it properly – dust in my eyes." Tom rubbed

at his eyes. Turning to Isis, he added, "But my friend here doesn't know *anything* about sailing."

Isis glared at Tom.

Magnus nodded and explained to Isis. "The crystal Erik's holding is called a sunstone. It reflects light, even on a cloudy day like this, so he can see where the sun is."

The gale blew harder and harder until Tom could barely keep his eyes open. The longship started to groan and creak. It was taking a real battering against the crashing waves. Terrified, Tom wondered if it would it hold together under the strain.

"HEAVE! HEAVE! HEAVE!" The rowers chanted, trying to push the boat forward against the headwind.

But the harder they rowed, the more the ship seemed to be tossed about like a carrot

in a massive cooking cauldron. Even Erik
had begun to look worried.

A wave crashed over the ship. Freezing-
cold spray showered over them, which felt
like icy needles.

"I don't want to die again!" Isis shrieked.

Tom could see she was wild-eyed with
fear.

"Don't worry, my child," said the grey-haired Geir, shrugging as the seawater dripped off his wiry eyebrows.

How can he be so calm? Tom wondered.

Suddenly, they felt the entire ship jolt against something hard. A horrible scraping noise came from the bottom of the hull.

"What's that?" Tom cried.

The wood started to creak as though it was being bent to its very limits. Tom clutched at the bench. He wondered if the ship was going to snap in two.

"We've hit rock bottom," Magnus said.

"You can say that again," Isis whimpered.

"Are we going to sink?" Tom asked.

The longship swung round and suddenly a rocky outcrop loomed before them. It reminded Tom of scary-looking teeth, reaching out to bite the ship in half.

"Drop anchor, men!" Erik bellowed. "We'll camp on this here island until the storm's blown over."

The Vikings grunted with effort but managed to steer the longship towards a strip of white sand. One surge of seawater pushed them into the tiny bay.

In the worst of the storm, Tom had pulled the hood of his cloak right down over his face. Now he dared to look up.

"Everybody out!" Erik said.

The Vikings sprang to their feet, snatching up rolls of cloth, rope and pegs from chests that were stowed beneath the benches. Within minutes, the outcrop swarmed with busy men, all pitching neat little tents in a perfect circle.

"Come on!" Magnus shouted over to Tom and Isis. "Hold the tent pegs while I knock them in. You can both share with me."

Isis flung back her hood and stumbled on wobbly sea legs over to the camp. "Me?

73

Share, with you two?" she sniffed.

"Suit yourself," Magnus said. "You can share with Bjørn the Bone-crusher, if you prefer. I hear he's got very cheesy feet because his boots leak, so there should be plenty of room in *his* tent."

Tom laughed. Isis glared at him, but then helped Magnus set up the tent. Soon the wind had died down a little and a fire was crackling. Everybody huddled round its flames, trying to warm up and dry their clothes. When Erik broke open a barrel of mead, the crew roared with delight. They filled their drinking horns to the brim.

"SKOL!" Magnus cheered, pushing a horn into Tom's hands. "Drink up! Like this..."

Magnus glugged the brew so thirstily that it streamed down his chin.

Tom sipped the thick, sickly sweet drink.

"Ugh!" he said. "Have a taste." He offered
the horn to Isis.

Isis sniffed it. "It smells... chewy."

Tom giggled. He held out his fingers
in front of the fire. "This is more like it,
though," he said. "I don't think I can take
much more of that icy water. I'm happy just
staying put on dry land for a while."

But as their fingers and toes thawed out, one by one, the men started to leave the camp and head back down to the beach.

"Where are they going?" Tom whispered to Isis.

"And what on earth are they doing?" Isis asked.

Magnus let out an enormous burp and wiped his mouth on the sleeve of his tunic. "Don't you realise? It's Saturday!" he cried. "Bath day, of course!"

Erik towered above their little group. He slammed down a meaty hand on Magnus's helmet and chuckled. "That's right, my boy! We Vikings have a reputation to keep up."

"Of being bloodthirsty murderers?" Tom said quietly.

Erik guffawed. "Naturally! But also..." he started to run his sausage-like fingers through his tangled red locks, "...the whole world knows a Viking takes pride in his lovely hair and how fresh he smells. Not like the English."

"What's wrong with the English?" Tom asked.

Erik suddenly grew serious. "I've heard," he began, "that the English never wash. And I mean, NEVER. In fact, when we land in England, don't be surprised if the smell knocks you out cold."

Isis snorted and looked at Tom with a raised eyebrow and a mischievous grin. "Yes, I've heard that, too," she said. "Englishmen smell like a dead horse's bottom. It's a fact."

"Dead horse's bottom! I *love* it!" Erik cried.

Erik and Magnus roared with laughter and slapped Isis hard on the back. Tom stuck out his tongue at her, but she was too gleeful to notice. He was just about to defend the fine scent of an Englishman when he remembered that he was supposed to be a Viking.

"Ha!" he said. "Ha ha ha!" He forced himself to laugh along. "Stinky, horse-pooey English people. Ha ha ha!"

But just to be on the safe side, he sniffed his armpits.

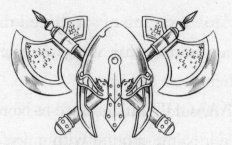

CHAPTER 6
SPELLING IT OUT

Bath time over, the Vikings returned to gather by the crackling fire. But that didn't mean their odd behaviour stopped there.

Tom watched, bewildered, as Erik heaved a lump of stone towards the fire. It was twice the size of his head, but covered with seaweed rather than red hair.

"Why has he picked up that boulder?" Isis asked. "Do you think he's going to smash it down on top of someone for fun?"

To their horror, Erik staggered right up to where they were sitting.

"NYAAAGH!" Erik grunted as he dropped the boulder to the ground with a *doof!*

Without saying a word, Erik flung himself down on to the sand and took out a short, sharp dagger.

"Help!" Tom said, cowering back.

Erik looked over at him. The firelight gave his craggy face scary shadows. *He looks more like a monster than a man*, Tom thought.

"This dagger isn't for you, boy," he said, chuckling.

Erik started to gouge out chunks from the boulder by digging the tip of his dagger into the surface of the stone. Shards of rock flew off in all directions and strange spiked shapes started to appear.

"I'm carving runes," he explained. "These symbols are magical. A stone with runes has the power to change the future."

"You're not planning on casting a nasty spell over us, are you?" Isis asked the huge Viking.

Erik grinned and stroked his beard thoughtfully. He pointed his dagger at her. "Not unless you really want me to. I know a good one that could turn you into a goat!"

Cleo crept out from under Isis's cloak, her fur standing on end.

"Don't worry, Fluffpot," Isis whispered, tickling her behind the ears. "It's the cold. It makes them crazy!"

Tom's curiosity overtook his fear. He scrambled closer to Erik to watch as the rock became covered in ancient letters. He wondered whether the runes said something about sailing safely across the ocean, or the Viking spirits protecting them.

"What does it say?" He asked, tingling with excitment.

Erik smiled and sheathed his dagger. He

blew the dust off the letters and ran his thumb proudly over his handiwork. "It says, 'May the Viking axes cut the English down like trees'."

Tom swallowed. What would Erik do to him if he ever found out he was English?

Erik patted the boulder and stood up quickly. He was so tall that Tom thought he looked like a tree – a huge old oak. As the Viking stretched, his arms were like great branches. His hair swung round his shoulders, like ivy scrambling down the trunk.

Erik grinned down at Tom. "But even though the runes' magic will help us, it doesn't mean you can slack off with your fighting!" His huge hand reached down and yanked the children to their feet.

Isis yelped.

Tom looked up into Erik's twinkling eyes.

"I expect each of my men to kill at least FIVE Englishmen," the Viking boomed. "And that includes you. It's the only way to ensure your place in Valhalla!"

Erik stomped away towards the barrel of mead.

Tom had no intention of killing anyone. He just wanted to find the amulet as quickly as possible, and escape before he and Isis got caught up in any violence.

"Five?" came a strangled voice at his side.

Magnus, who'd been eavesdropping, had turned a sickly shade of grey. He was tugging at his plaits nervously.

"You were boasting about looting earlier," Isis said to him. Her black eyebrows were knitted together in a frown. "You said you were excited. So what's wrong now, Mr Tough Guy?!"

Magnus just put his head in his hands and groaned.

Tom pulled Isis to one side by her elbow. "Hey, stop teasing him. We need to concentrate on the amulet. Did you notice what Erik said?"

Isis nodded. "Valhalla," she said. "It was in the riddle, wasn't it? Another clue! Do you know what Valhalla is?"

Tom rubbed his chin. "I'm not sure," he said. "But it does sound familiar, like some kind of warriors' hall of fame, or something. Let me have a think..."

He looked up at the starry sky and racked his brains for all the history facts he had stored there. It was like rummaging through a big box of Lego, looking for exactly the right piece. But as hard as he tried he couldn't remember what Valhalla was.

"Nope. Not a clue," he said, shaking his head.

Isis turned to the young Viking, and tapped him on the helmet.

"Hey! What's Valhalla?" she asked.

Magnus looked up and stared at Isis in disbelief. "It's the place where all brave Vikings go when they die, of course. An afterlife for warriors." He started to smile. "A banqueting hall where you feast forever, and drink and fight with the gods themselves. Imagine that!"

The colour flushed back into Magnus's cheeks and his smile broadened into a delighted grin as he thought about Valhalla. Just then, Erik stomped back, mead sloshing from the horn in his hand.

"Talking about – *hic* – Valhalla – *hic*?" Erik hiccupped, lifting the mead to his mouth. He missed and poured some down his matted red moustache. "You'd better make sure you kill five Englishmen as soon as you land, *hic*!" he said, swaying slightly. "That way, if you get killed yourself, you'll go straight there."

The scent of stewing meat wafted over from the cooking pot. But even the comforting smell didn't make Tom feel any less fearful.

"Thanks for the advice, Erik," he said, meekly.

The ground started to rumble beneath him. At first Tom wondered if it was his stomach growling. But Isis gripped his arm and Cleo scratched at the ground with her razor-sharp claws.

"Anubis!" Isis whispered.

Tom scanned the camp, trying to spot the god's dog-head. Where was he?

"The cooking pot!" Isis gasped in horror.

Sure enough, Anubis's head popped out of the stew. His eyes flickered in the fire's flames like burning coals. His black muzzle stuck out like a lump of charred wood.

"PAH!" he scoffed. "Valhalla doesn't exist. I'm the god of the Underworld, so I should know!"

Isis strode towards the fire and threw her hands in the air. "What do you want? You gave us a mission and we're doing it. Why do you have to stick your snout into everything?"

Tom thought she was being even more cheeky than usual.

Anubis bared his long, sharp teeth. "I've come to tell you that these hairy heathens are right about one thing."

"Oh, yes? What's that then, Your Dogliness?!" Isis asked.

Anubis sniggered cruelly and vanished in a puff of black smoke. All that remained in the cooking pot was the greasy, meaty stew. But his booming voice echoed on the wind:

"Get ready to die on the mainland!"

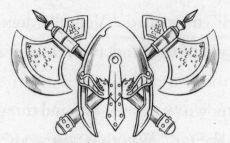

CHAPTER 7
LAND AHOY!

"Back on board the boat, you lot!" Erik's gruff voice came from outside.

Tom's eyes flickered open. He felt cold, hard ground beneath him. He saw the cloth of the tent above him and heard snoring right by his head. It was morning.

"Pack up! It's time to go!" ordered Erik.

Tom scrambled to his knees. In the murky light, he saw Isis. She was sleeping with her hands crossed over her chest. Cleo was curled up at her feet. Next to her, taking up so much of the tent that his feet stuck right out of the flap, was a snoring Magnus.

Tom shook them both roughly awake. Isis stretched and rubbed her almond-shaped brown eyes.

"Where are we?" she asked. She looked over at Magnus. "Yuck. What a sight to wake up to. Oh, I remember now. We've got to get back on to that horrid little tub of a boat."

Cleo meowed mournfully. She looked so scared that even Tom wanted to pick her up and cuddle her.

They trudged down to the sandy bay. Standing on a black rock, with his red hair blowing in the breeze, was Erik the Red.

"Come on, you two! Stop dragging your heels and get on board," he said. He pointed

up at the weak sunshine streaming through
the grey clouds. "See? My runes have
brought us good sailing weather."

Tom looked at the longship, which was already crammed full of enormous, hairy men. He groaned. Isis moaned. Cleo took one look at the boat's mast, which was now sopping wet from the storm, and hissed.

"You can sit on my lap, Fluffpot," Isis said, picking up her cat.

With his plaits swinging round his shoulders, Bjørn the Bone-crusher hung out of the boat and offered Isis a rough hand.

The princess stopped short as the foaming seawater licked the soles of her boots. "Do we really have to?" she asked Tom.

"Just think of the amulet," Tom whispered.

Sighing, Isis climbed on to the boat.

Tom turned to Erik. "How much longer before we get to England?" he asked.

Erik took off his helmet and scratched his

tangled hair. "Two days, by my reckoning."

As Tom and Isis took their places, squished in between Magnus and Geir, a group of the burliest Vikings pushed the boat fully into the water, hopping in at the very last moment.

"Take your oars, men!" Erik cried. "Let's go, Vikings!"

The sea was calm. They sailed all through the day and into the freezing, starlit night. On the following morning, Tom noticed that Erik was standing at the front of the boat again. The Viking captain was squinting at something on the horizon. A thin, black line. From under a bench, he pulled out a cage. It contained three squawking crows. He let them loose.

In a flurry of black feathers, the beady-eyed crows flapped off towards the dark line in the distance.

"Land ahoy!" Erik shouted. "Follow the crows, lads!"

"Land?" Tom said, nudging Isis. "And early too!"

As the rhythm of the oars drew them ever closer to the coast, Tom started to see looming cliffs. Crowned with grassy moorland, they looked as though they had sprouted straight out of the water. On top of the cliffs were castle-like buildings. From the crosses on their roofs, Tom guessed they might be monasteries.

"SCOTLAND!" Erik suddenly shouted. "Or at least, a Scottish isle. The wind has blown us a little off course, lads. But the pickings here will be just as rich as in England, and with fewer people to put up a fight."

The Vikings all started to cheer with a

deafening roar. "HOORAH! HOORAH! HOORAH!"

The longship sailed into shallower waters, and Erik gave the order to drop anchor. Men scrambled to untie the little landing boats, which were lashed to the sides of the longship with thick ropes.

Tom peered up into the grassy hills that hugged the bay. Dotted in small clusters were little stone cottages with thatched roofs. He could see smoke curling upwards from the chimneys. They were so different from the simple wooden roundhouses he and Isis had seen in King Arthur's England, just four hundred years earlier.

"Into the boats!" Erik ordered the men, thrusting an iron broadsword, a round shield and a sheathed dagger at each of the crew.

"Kill five for Valhalla, remember?" he

said, patting each man on the shoulder.

Tom, Isis, Cleo and Magnus were the last to leave the longship. Magnus looked as deathly pale as his white-blond hair. He hopped into one of the little boats and grabbed two sets of oars.

"We'll row together, Tom," Magnus said, offering Tom a pair of oars. "Cat-girl can sit and give orders. I think she'll prefer that."

Isis flung herself on to the bench at the back and sat regally, with Cleo on her lap.

As Tom pulled on the oars, struggling to keep up with Magnus's pace, Isis had a jolly time doing the thing she loved most: being bossy.

"Left a bit! No! Right a bit!" she ordered. "Faster! The others have already landed."

Tom slumped over his oars and groaned.

"Would you like a go? Because you obviously you think you can do better."

"Don't be ridiculous," Isis scoffed. "I'm the brains of this operation."

"Funny, that," Tom whispered. "Because I could have sworn you'd had your brains pulled out through your nostrils five thousand years ago."

Isis's face crumpled up in outrage. But before she could reply, a voice called, "Get off our island!"

At the water's edge, some ragged-looking villagers waved sticks and knives at the Vikings. The men wore dark blue and green kilts, with animal-skin cloaks draped round their shoulders. Like the Vikings, the Scots' hair was long but it wasn't nicely braided. It was a shaggy mess, as were their beards. The women wore simple, long dresses and scarves on their heads. They looked almost as fierce as the men.

Erik was standing on the beach, directing his men up towards the village. He shouted to them, "You have nothing to fear from these Scots!"

The Vikings answered with a noisy cheer. They waved their swords in the air. Tom's arms and legs seemed to have turned to mush.

One of the Scots threw a spear at the invaders, as his fellow islanders let out a battle cry.

Erik bashed his sword hilt on his helmet. "Take no notice, lads!" he cried. "They can't scare us – we're Viking warriors, the toughest in the world!" He beckoned the stragglers, who were still rowing their boats towards the shore. "Come out of your boats fighting! I want everyone in this village dead by the end of the day."

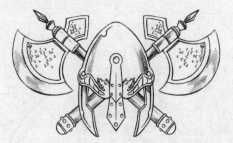

CHAPTER 8
LOOTING AND PILLAGING

"AAARGH! Feel Thor's hammer coming down on your heads!" Bjørn the Bone-crusher yelled, as he sprinted at the villagers.

Five or six Vikings followed behind him, waving their axes and swords in the air with big, hairy arms.

"Death to the Scots!" they cried.

Even from a distance, Tom could see how the villagers' faces had paled. They still

prodded their sticks and pitchforks at the Viking invaders, but he noticed they were stepping backwards up the path.

Isis covered her eyes. "I can't bear to watch," she said. She covered Cleo's eyes with the edge of her cloak. "Don't look, Fluffpot. You'll get nightmares."

Tom looked over at Magnus. He seemed
to be rowing along the shore, rather than
towards the land. His eyes were fixed
nervously on the struggle between the
Scots and the Viking crew. The clang of
clashing metal was carried all the way
down to the sea.

"What's the matter?" Tom asked gently.

Magnus shook his head and trailed his oar in the shallow water.

"I don't want to fight," he said. "I'm so ashamed. I thought I'd be able to, but I suppose I'm just not that kind of a Viking."

Tom sighed heavily. "Me, neither. The last thing I want to do is kill a bunch of poor Scottish villagers. They've done nothing wrong."

"Well, we can't just hang about here!" Isis said, grabbing an oar off Tom. "Even if we're not a bunch of bloodthirsty lunatics, Erik and his men are. And they'll kill us if they think we're cowards. So we have to get on that island and see this thing through. DON'T WE?"

She mouthed the word, 'amulet' at Tom and jabbed her finger towards the shore.

Then she started to row so haphazardly, that the boat and its occupants were soon dripping wet.

Realising she was right, Tom grabbed back the oar and started to row the boat to shore in earnest.

"Come on, Magnus. We'll find a way to stay out of the battle," he promised, as the boat pulled up on the beach.

Out of the corner of his eye, Tom could see that the villagers were fleeing into the hills in earnest. Their screams carried on the wind. Even the very young and the very old were running away from the Vikings as fast as they could.

"Get after them, men!" Erik cried, waving his axe. "Give them a Viking lesson they won't forget." His eyes were wild and his red hair looked like it was on fire. He seemed to

be in some kind of battle frenzy. *No wonder the Vikings stomped all over Britain,* Tom thought. *I bet people died from heart attacks before these guys had even drawn blood.*

Erik noticed Tom, Isis, Cleo and Magnus lagging behind.

"Get up to the village," he shouted. "You can start looting!" He started issuing more orders. "Search every house. Be on the lookout for jewellery and gold. What you can carry, steal. Anything else, BURN!"

Erik punched the air and growled. Then

he sprinted off after his other men, shouting, "Forward! Forward! Men of Thor!"

"We have to look as if we're doing something," Tom said to Magnus. "But no burning, OK?"

They trudged through the hillside to the village.

Magnus nodded. "Agreed. We'll be OK if we stick together," he said, mustering a half-smile.

The first house they came to was a wooden hut, rather than one of the stone cottages they had seen from the sea. The walls were buckled outwards and the roof was covered in chunks of grass and mud. The door hung crookedly on its hinges. Tom held his breath, hoping that a Scottish peasant wasn't going to jump out and attack them with a pitchfork.

Luckily, the hut seemed to be empty. "I think we've walked into some kind of store cupboard," Isis said, poking at a pile of nets and hooks. She held her nose. "It smells like the time I shoved a sardine into the High Priest's headdress on a hot summer's day."

Tom could see nothing in the shadows but simple furniture and fishing equipment. In a corner was a thick pile of straw, half-covered with a dirty sheepskin.

"This is a poor fisherman's home," he said. "There's nothing of value in here. Let's go."

Magnus nodded, turned on his heel and left the hut, ready to move on to the next house. But Isis carried on pushing things aside with her toes, or with her hand wrapped in her cloak.

"No, Tom. We should definitely still look. You never know, DO YOU?" She grabbed him and whispered loudly in his ear. "The amulet could be anywhere. So we have to look EVERYWHERE."

Suddenly, there was a loud rustle, followed by a crackling noise.

"What was that?" Tom said, looking round the hut in fear and holding his sword out in front of him.

"Over there!" Isis said.

In a corner of the hut was a pile of ragged clothes, stacked high against the wall. The clothes twitched.

Tom reached forward and flicked the top layer of clothing on to the floor.

"AAAAAARRRGGGH!" shrieked two heads, popping out suddenly from underneath the pile of rags.

"AAAAARRRGGGH!" shouted Tom
and Isis, scuttling several steps back towards
the door.

Tom took a closer look at the heads, and
realised they belonged to children.

He clapped a hand over Isis's mouth. "Shh! We're frightening them," he said. Tom thought the boy looked about four, and the girl about two. The children suddenly burst into tears.

Oh no! thought Tom. He had no idea what to do. Thinking fast, he started singing 'Twinkle Twinkle Little Star'.

The children stopped crying and giggled.

"Look, the kiddies are cute," said Isis impatiently. "But we're not here to babysit. We need to find that amulet."

"I've got an idea!" Tom said brightly. "Let's just pretend to loot this house. We'll look for the amulet while we're doing it."

For the next ten minutes, Tom and Isis stayed in the safety of the fisherman's hut, searching through everything. They made as much noise as possible, throwing things about, so that anybody passing would think they were happily looting.

The children seemed to think it was a game, and ran round the hut kicking the furniture and knocking things down. Tom didn't have the heart to tell them that their village was actually under siege.

Before long, Tom heard the sound of "HOORAH! HOORAH!" carrying on the wind. He groaned. He was pretty sure he knew whose voice it was.

"Erik!" he and Isis said at the same time.

CHAPTER 9
VALHALLA BOUND

"Stay here and hide," Tom whispered to the children.

Tom and Isis walked out of the hut. Magnus came over to them.

"Phew!" said Isis, wiping her brow. "Looting sure is a tiring business."

Tom played along. "I've never pillaged so much before in my life."

"I want anything made of metal," Erik

shouted. "Remember! Gold, bronze or iron. It can all be melted down once we're home. Anything shiny - jewels, resin, polished bone."

Tom scoured the village for another house they could pretend to loot until the horrible business was over.

"Hey! Look at Geir! He's clutching at his stomach," Tom said, pointing to the grey-haired warrior. The old Viking was bent double over a large, dark-red stain on his clothing.

Geir came stumbling towards them. His face had turned a deathly white. His eyes were scrunched up in pain.

"What happened to you?" Magnus asked, as he ran to meet his crewmate.

Geir collapsed into his arms.

"T-took a pitch fork to the belly," he stuttered.

Blood seeped from between his fingers as he clutched at his wound.

Magnus turned to Tom with a frightened look in his eyes. "We've got to find somewhere comfortable for him."

"Take him to the fisherman's hut!" Tom suggested. "Me and Isis can get some water."

Magnus nodded. As he led Geir into the fisherman's hut, Tom and Isis picked up a bronze bucket that somebody had filled with loot. They emptied the valuables on to the grass and dashed over to a well that was in the middle of the village. When they had filled the bucket, they ran back to Magnus with the sloshing contents.

"Boo!" cried the two toddlers, popping up from under the sheepskin.

"Who are they?" Magnus asked in surprise.

"They're just kids – I told them to hide here," Tom explained.

"Well, tell them to run away," warned Magnus. "Erik will be here any minute. He's going round the houses, inspecting them."

Magnus took the cleanest cloth he could find from the clothes pile and soaked it in water. He squeezed some drops into Geir's mouth.

"I'm going to V-Valhalla, you know," Geir said in a croaky voice. He grabbed Magnus's arm. "Make sure they give me a good Viking send-off."

"Don't talk such rubbish. You're going to be fine," Magnus said, pressing the wet cloth to Geir's wound.

Tom could hear Erik slamming doors as he inspected a nearby house. He knew there was no time to lose.

Tom kneeled down in front of the two little kids. "We're going to play a new game now, OK?"

They looked at him with wide eyes.

"Put these sheepskins over you. Pretend you're lambs. When I say 'Go!' I want you to run as fast as you can up into the hills so the Big Bad Wolf can't get you. Understand?"

They nodded eagerly. Tom led them to the door and waited.

Moments later, the door was smashed open against the wall.

"What's going on in here?!" Erik stood in the doorway with his hands on his hips.

"Go!" hissed Tom, pushing out the two children.

"What in Thor's name was that?" Erik boomed.

"Just some sheep!" Tom lied. "Those Scots keep their animals in the house with them!"

Erik spat on the floor. "Disgusting!" he said, shaking his head. He looked round the hut. "What are you doing wasting your time in here? There's nothing worth looting in this dump."

"We're tending to Geir," Isis explained. "He's badly wounded."

Erik's red eyebrows shot up to his hairline. "If Geir dies, at least he fought like a warrior." He pointed a finger at the door. "Get out there and start looting."

Reluctantly, Tom, Isis and Magnus joined the rest of the Vikings, who were running from house to house, smashing everything in their path, hoping to find more treasure.

"At least most of the villagers managed to get away," Tom whispered to Isis.

Isis nodded and whispered back, "The Egyptians were strict rulers. My father didn't manage to build pyramids by being a cuddly kitten," she said. "But he would never let his men run around looting and pillaging. This is just terrible."

"TERRIBLE? What's terrible?" Erik bellowed suddenly.

Isis jumped. Her eyes darted to and fro, as though she was choosing the right words to say. "I was just saying, er, that the Scots' belongings are a pile of terrible rubbish." She kicked over a stool for emphasis.

When Erik had stomped off again, Tom said, "We'd better pretend to loot. If we don't, we'll end up salted in a barrel and served up for dinner on their journey home."

Tom and Isis ran in and out of houses grabbing random items, doing their best to look like they were looting. In fact, what they were really doing was looking for the amulet. But before they had a chance to search every house, Erik appeared in the doorway of the village church.

"Get yourselves in here, lads!" he shouted. He lifted a beautifully carved Celtic cross above his head and smashed it into smithereens on the ground. "There are statues here that need pounding to rubble." He started to jump up and down on the broken pieces of cross.

"That's terrible!" gasped Tom. He couldn't believe that the Vikings, who had their own gods, could be so disrespectful of other people's beliefs.

Isis blinked hard and flicked her plaits dramatically. "Are you going to stand up to *that*?" She pointed at Erik.

Tom looked at the giant Viking, who was pounding his axe on the broken stones until they were dust. Erik was in such a bloodthirsty frenzy, Tom felt certain that if he approached him, Erik would crush him to dust too! He swallowed hard. "OK. Maybe not."

Dusk sucked the light out of the sky and left shadows all about. The village smelled of burned wood, briny sea air, and sorrow. Even the gulls returning to their nests glided along in silence. The Vikings had invaded a lively little fishing village and had left behind a ghost town.

Mercifully, Tom noted that the looting seemed to have come to an end. As the Viking crew gathered round the well and drank from its water, Erik trudged out of the fisherman's hut. All eyes were on him.

"How is he? Does Geir live?" Magnus asked.

Erik turned solemnly to the crew and removed his helmet. "Geir has died. His battle wounds were beyond our healing powers."

Everybody looked at their boots and muttered words of sadness and grief.

But Erik clambered on top of the well and stood up. "Don't be downhearted, lads! Geir has gone to Valhalla." He slapped his thighs and shouted, "HOORAH!"

Suddenly, everyone seemed cheered by this. "HOORAH! HOORAH! HOORAH!" they yelled with delight. "Geir is fighting and feasting with the gods!"

"Be on the shore at dawn, lads," Erik said, tugging at his long red hair. "We'll give Geir a hero's burial!"

Ear-splitting cheering almost knocked
Tom off his feet.

He looked at Isis. "Why on earth are
they so happy?" he asked. "Aren't funerals
supposed to be sad?" Tom felt sorry for Geir
– the old man had been kind to him, and he
felt sad that the warrior had passed away
in such pain.

Isis shrugged. "Not in Egypt. We have the
Afterlife to look forward to."

"So how's that working out for you?"
Tom asked.

Isis stuck out her tongue at him.

Magnus beamed at them. "We're pleased
because Geir is going to heroes' heaven.
He'll be put on a boat loaded with treasure,
and then set on fire so he can go to Valhalla.
Death doesn't get better than that!"

Amidst the frenzied celebrations, Tom

pulled Isis and Cleo aside. "You know what this means, don't you?" he asked Isis.

Isis's eyes shone in the dusky light. "Yes, I remember! The riddle said, *Their souls for Valhalla yearn!*"

"Exactly," Tom said, clutching his cloak close against the early evening cold – or was it just a chill of excitement? "The riddle mentioned a *flaming arrow* trained on a boat. That must be what Magnus was talking about."

"And the last line was about being, *sure that jewel won't burn.*" Isis snatched up Cleo and held her close. "Oh, Fluffpot. We're almost there! We'll be in the Afterlife soon!"

CHAPTER 10
VIKING FUNERAL

Tom, Isis and Magnus spent the night in a cottage hidden from view. They snuggled into a pile of straw and sheepskins and had a good night's sleep. The sun was just a smudgy streak of pink on the grey horizon when they made their way down to the beach.

The entire crew of the Viking longship was gathered for the funeral. They listened with grave, hard faces to the prayers that

Erik said. The waves crashed against the rocks further along the coast, but the bay itself was calm. The sand was covered in a beautiful layer of glittering morning frost.

"...And lo! His forefathers are calling Geir to join them, bidding him to take his place in the halls of Valhalla, where forever the brave do live," Erik said in a serious voice, dipping his chin on to his chest.

Tom and Isis snuck forwards to get a clearer view of Geir's funeral boat. The warrior's body had been laid in the middle and he was dressed in a clean tunic, leather trousers, a beaver-skin cloak and his helmet. In one hand, he held a sword. In the other, over his chest, he held a shield.

"What's all that stuff in the boat with him?" Isis asked.

Tom squinted hard in the gloomy dawn

light. He could see daggers in their leather sheaths, an axe, some shining armour and plates of fruit, meat and bread that had been plundered from the Scottish village.

"It's everything he'll need in the next life," Magnus said.

"Oh, good," Isis said. "It's important to be prepared for the Afterlife." She whispered to Tom, "Although I was buried with *much* nicer things than that."

"Yes, but at least Geir hasn't had his guts removed and shoved into jars," Tom said.

Isis tutted. "It didn't do me any harm!" she said.

Suddenly, something dazzling and bright caught Tom's eye.

"Hey!" he said to Isis. "I think there's jewellery too. Let's get a closer look."

Creeping forward, Tom and Isis spotted

a necklace, hanging from the tip of a sword.
Set into the centre of it was...

"The pink amulet!" Isis said, turning to
Tom with excitement.

When Erik had finished chanting Viking
prayers and poetry, the men started to push
the boat towards the gently lapping sea.

They heaved and grunted and harrumphed, scrabbling to keep their footing in the damp sand. Finally, rolling the vessel over logs they had found in the woods, the boat made contact with the beginning of water that stretched up the beach. "Farewell, Geir!" the men shouted.

"Oh, no!" Isis gasped. "The boat's sailing away!"

"We need to do something quick!" Tom said. But unfortunately, he had no idea what that might be. "What happens next?" he asked Magnus in panic.

Magnus wiped a tear from his pale eyelashes and sniffed hard. "When the boat has drifted well away from the shore, someone will fire a flaming arrow into it."

"To set the boat on fire?" Tom asked.

"Yes," Magnus said. "The whole vessel

will burn, and the ashes of Geir's body, the things in there with him – all of it will be swallowed by the sea."

Tom looked at Isis. Isis looked at Tom. They nodded – then ran!

Tom and Isis dashed up the beach to where the landing boats were moored. Tom fiddled with the ropes that tied them together. His hands were numb with cold as he worked at the knot.

"Hurry up!" Isis shouted.

Tom looked over his shoulder. The boat carrying Geir was drifting further and further from the shore. Gulls circled overhead. "Got it!" he cried, as the knot finally came undone.

"Help me, or we're going to lose the amulet," Tom told Isis.

Together, they tugged the little boat on to the sea and started rowing. Amazingly, given how rubbish Isis was at rowing, they soon caught up with Geir's boat.

"Get away from there, you fools!" Erik bellowed from the beach. He looked furious as he watched Tom and Isis pull alongside the funeral boat. The Viking named Bjørn was beginning to light the tip of his arrow with a flaming torch.

"Just keep going," Tom said.

Isis stretched out her arm. "I can almost touch it," she said gleefully.

But just as she was within a fingertip's reach of the funeral boat, a huge swell of water, almost four metres high, rose up from the seabed. Tom let out a desperate groan as it pushed them out of reach of Geir's boat. The freak wave put an impossible distance between their boat and Geir's.

"WHOOPS!" rumbled a voice on the wind.

Cleo's fur stood to attention in stiff spikes.

A deep-throated chuckling rose up from under the waves.

"Anubis!" Isis said. "What a troublemaker!"

"We can't give up now!" Tom said. "Keep rowing!"

"I can't carry on much longer!" Isis moaned. "Princesses aren't really used to this kind of work!"

She wasn't the only one struggling. Tom let go of his oars to examine his stinging palms. He winced. The skin on his hands was blistered and raw.

"We can't give up," he said. "There's just a couple more metres to go."

Gritting his teeth with determination, Tom heaved his oars against the flow of water until, at last, they drew next to the other boat. He grabbed the side and loosely tied their boat to Geir's with a length of rope.

"Hurry!" he said, flinging himself into the funeral boat.

Tom stretched out a helping hand to Isis, but she ignored him and leaped nimbly across by herself.

Cleo peered over the side into the dark water, and took a step back, hissing.

"I don't think she wants to risk another wetting," Isis said. "Poor darling. We'll just be a minute, Cleo. Now, where is that amulet?"

Tom and Isis rummaged frantically through the jewellery that lay strewn about the boat.

"Aha!" cried Tom, holding up the necklace proudly.

Isis snatched it from his hand. "Perfect!" she cried. "Now, let's get out of here."

"I warned you two!" Erik yelled.

Looking out across the water, Tom could see how angry Erik was – his red face matched his hair.

"And now you're stealing from my dead warrior," he roared, shaking his fist at them.

"You've gone too far! I'll not delay this funeral any longer. Geir could use a couple of servants in Valhalla. Prepare to burn!"

Tom saw the Viking turn to Bjørn and give him an instruction. Bjørn nocked the flaming arrow against his bow.
He aimed towards the boat.

The released arrow went off course in a gust of wind and fizzled harmlessly on the surface of the water ten metres away.

"That was a bit of luck!" Isis said. "Come on… hurry!"

Clutching the amulet necklace in her hand, she scrambled over the treasure and jumped back to the safety of their little boat.

But Tom was frozen with fear. He watched as Bjørn aimed yet another flaming arrow at the boat. This time, it sped up, up, up into the sky with a flaming, golden tail. And then it whizzed back down… straight towards Geir's boat.

"AAAARGH!" Tom cried, as the arrow found its mark in the hull.

The arrow splintered a plank with a *thud!* And then the hungry fire claimed its wooden feast.

Roaring flames sprang up and Tom could feel the heat against his face.

"Don't just stand there!" shouted Isis, snapping Tom out of his terrified trance. The flames were getting too close for comfort now. She started untying the little boat from the flaming funeral boat. "Jump!" she urged him.

Tom knew he had to jump, or else be fried alive in his very own Viking barbecue.

I am NOT going to sizzle like a sausage, he thought.

Tom sprang over the side – but the little boat had drifted too far away.

Splash!

"Klaflooffla!" Tom said, as his mouth and nose filled with cold, salty water. His heavy, waterlogged cloak was pulling him down, down, down into the freezing, inky water.

He went under. The
men shouting on the
shore, Isis screaming,
and the crackle of the
burning boat suddenly
all fell silent. The only
thing Tom could
hear was his own
heart thumping as
he sank.

I can't drown, he
thought. *Isis will never
get her other amulets.*

Tom started to
kick his legs with all
the strength he could
muster. At the same
time, he shrugged off
his heavy fur cloak.

Just when he thought his lungs might explode, he broke the surface, gasping for air.

"Swim, Tom! Swim!" Isis screeched.

Finally, he started to do his best front crawl towards Isis, remembering to breathe to the side and keep his kicking legs straight. *My swimming teacher would be proud*, he thought.

He quickly covered the distance between Geir's funeral inferno and their landing boat. He grabbed the side and Isis hauled him into safety. Tom collapsed in the bottom of the boat, dripping and shivering.

"OW!" He looked down at his toe and saw that Cleo had just nipped him. "What was that for? I nearly drowned."

Isis grabbed a set of oars and rolled her eyes at Tom. "You trod on her tail, you clumsy boy!"

Before Tom had a chance to reply, Geir's boat made a sizzling noise.

He turned round and saw that the flames had greedily gobbled up everything, right down to the foamy surface of the water. Only a few planks of charred wood remained, and then they, too, sank to the bottom of the North Sea, taking the ashes of Geir with them.

"Goodbye, brave Geir," Tom said solemnly. "I hope you make it safely to Valhalla."

"Goodbye," Isis said, sniffing.

Then Tom stood and took Cleo's paw in one hand and Isis's hand in the other. "Come on," he said, shivering. "I'm freezing. It's time to go home."

As all three of them touched the pink amulet, a tornado whipped round their legs.

Tom felt himself being sucked up into the tunnels of time. With eyes clamped shut, the three friends shot round the bends, twists and turns through history.

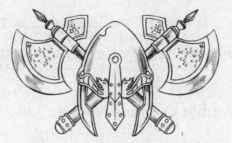

CHAPTER 11
BACK TO THE FILM

"Wheeeee!" Tom shouted. "This is better than being tossed on the high seas!"

"And it doesn't smell of fish!" Isis cried.

"Meow!" said Cleo, sounding a little disappointed.

They were catapulted back to modern-day England. Tom landed in his cinema seat with such an almighty *thunk!* he felt his teeth to check they hadn't been knocked clean out. Isis and Cleo landed beside him. *Flump! Flump!* Both were in their mummies' wrappings once again.

"We're back," Tom said, looking up at the flickering screen. "And the film is right where we left it."

On the screen, the hero was grappling with the baddie on the roof of a skyscraper. The baddie knocked the weapon out of the hero's hand, and pushed him closer and closer to the roof's edge.

"Ooh, goody!" Isis said, bouncing in her seat. "This is exciting!"

Tom sighed. He'd had quite enough excitement for one day. In real life, he'd just taken part in a Viking raid and very nearly burned to death on a funeral boat. That was a million times more exciting than what was happening on the screen.

But before he'd even had a chance to recover from his Viking adventure, Tom's seat started to rumble and the curtains on either side of the cinema screen started flapping again.

"Uh oh!" Tom said. "Looks like there's more drama ahead…"

"Honestly," Isis grumbled. "Why can't he wait until the end of the film? I want to find out what happens…"

Tom groaned loudly as the jackal-headed god burst out of the cinema screen, more terrifying than any movie baddie. "I don't think Anubis wants us to have a happy ending," he muttered to Isis.

"Shh," hissed the man sitting behind Tom. "If you don't stop talking I'm going to get the manager."

The man obviously couldn't see the

enormous Egyptian god towering at the
front of the cinema, his red eyes narrowed
in anger.

"Where's my amulet!" Anubis growled
so loudly that Tom covered his ears and
slumped down in his seat. The god loomed
over the rows of seats and snarled at Isis,
showering Tom with a spray of doggy
slobber.

Isis dangled the necklace from her
fingertip. The pink stone caught the light
from the film projector and twinkled in
the dark.

"I don't think you deserve it," she said.
"The big wave you caused just wasn't
playing fair."

"HA!" The god of the Underworld
laughed humourlessly. "I'll tell you what's
not playing fair – hiding the amulet that was

rightfully MINE. You got yourself into this situation, Princess Isis. So don't come crying to me about what's fair."

Anubis snatched the amulet from her. He greedily examined the pink stone, baring his sharp teeth as he growled in satisfaction.

"I'm surprised those hairy Vikings didn't tear you to pieces and throw you on the bonfire," the god admitted.

"Guess you underestimated us," Isis said smugly, crossing her bandaged arms over her chest.

"Don't underestimate ME!" Anubis boomed. "I obviously haven't made these adventures hard enough—"

"You have," Tom interrupted. "Trust me, you have!"

"Silence, boy!" Anubis shouted. "Since you're finding these missions so easy, I'll be sure to send you somewhere more DANGEROUS next time!" Chuckling ominously, the god vanished as suddenly as he had appeared.

Tom turned to Isis. "Why can't you ever hold your tongue?" he said.

"Why can't YOU hold your tongue," the man sitting behind them said angrily. "You're ruining the film for us!"

Tom settled back into his chair and watched the rest of the film in silence. Soon, the theme music started playing and the credits rolled. Tom blinked as the house lights came on.

"Well, how did you like your first trip to the cinema?" Tom asked Isis, ignoring the glares he was getting from the man sitting behind him.

"It was... BRILLIANT!" she said. "I wish we'd had movies back when I was alive."

Cleo, who was gobbling up spilled popcorn from the floor, meowed in agreement.

Tom smiled. Isis didn't usually admit that Ancient Egypt wasn't perfect.

As they walked out of the cinema, Isis stopped to stare at the posters for upcoming films. One poster featured aliens coming out of a spaceship, another showed a cowboy.

"Ooh! Can we go and see this one!" she squealed, pointing to a poster of a vampire.

"Maybe," said Tom. Movies were fun, but he was more excited about their next time-travel adventure. So far, they'd been to Ancient Rome, King Arthur's England and the land of the Vikings. He knew that wherever Anubis sent them next would feature more danger and action than any movie.

And Tom couldn't wait!

TIME HUNTERS

TURN THE PAGE TO . . .

→ Meet the REAL Vikings!

→ Find out fantastic FACTS!

→ Battle with your GAMING CARDS!

→ And MUCH MORE!

WHO WERE THE MIGHTIEST VIKINGS?

Erik the Red was a *real* Viking! Find out more about him and other fearsome Vikings.

IVAR THE BONELESS was a Viking leader who ruled parts of Denmark and Sweden. No one knows for sure why he got his name – some people believe he had an illness that made the bones in his legs soft, so that he had to be carried around on shields. Even if this was true, it didn't stop him from invading England in AD 865! He must have been a fierce warrior.

VIKINGS

IVAR the BONELESS

Brain Power	320
Fear Factor	190
Bravery	310
Weapon: Bow and Arrow	210

— TOTAL **1030** —

ERIK THE RED is thought to have got his nickname because he had red hair. But it might have been because of his temper…

He was thrown out of Iceland after killing two of his neighbours. He travelled across the sea and discovered a cold, icy land, which he called Greenland. He convinced other Vikings to move there, and the settlement grew to

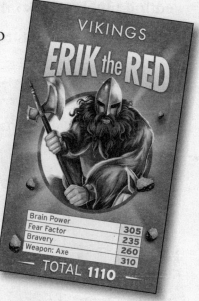

5,000 people. In AD 1002 a new group of immigrants brought over a disease which killed many of the settlers, including Erik the Red. Erik's son, Leif Erikson, was also a great explorer – he was the first Viking to reach North America.

HARALD BLUETOOTH was King of Denmark from AD 958. According to legend, he got the name Bluetooth because he liked eating blueberries so much that they stained his teeth! During his reign he ordered the

VIKINGS
HARALD BLUETOOTH

Brain Power	
Fear Factor	240
Bravery	200
Weapon: Sword	230
	220

— TOTAL **890** —

building of many forts and bridges. Harold died in battle in AD 986, fighting against rebel forces led by his son, Sweyn Forkbeard. Now that isn't a nice way to treat your dad, is it?

CANUTE THE GREAT was a Danish king. His army invaded England in AD 1013 and by 1016 Canute was the King of England as well. He didn't stop there – over the next twelve years he became king of Denmark, Norway and parts of Sweden! Even though Canute had invaded England, he was a popular and successful king as he respected old laws and was seen as a fair ruler.

VIKINGS
CANUTE the GREAT

Brain Power	360
Fear Factor	400
Bravery	350
Weapon: Spear	360
—TOTAL 1470—	

WEAPONS

Vikings often sailed to foreign shores and raided towns and villages for gold and weapons. They were terrifying fighters and used lots of different weapons when they attacked.

Viking Sword: handed down from generations. Made from iron and steel and usually double-edged. Sword handles were decorated in gold or silver.

Spear: a common, cheap weapon. It had an iron blade and a wooden shaft and was usually two to three metres long.

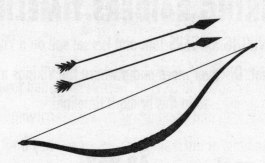

Bow and arrows: used to attack an enemy from a distance, or for hunting.

Battle axe: so sharp that they could cut through helmets and shields.

Chain mail: worn by richer Vikings who could afford to pay for extra protection.

VIKING RAIDERS TIMELINE

In VIKING RAIDERS Tom and Isis set sail on a Viking longboat. Discover more about where the Vikings travelled to in this brilliant timeline!

AD 789
Vikings begin their attacks on England.

AD 862
Vikings founded the city of Novgorod in Russia.

AD 900
Vikings raids along the Mediterranean coast.

AD 840
Vikings settlers founded the city of Dublin in Ireland.

AD 874
Vikings settle in Iceland.

It's freezing!

AD 1010 Viking settlement of Vinland in north America is founded.

AD 1028 King Canute conquers Norway.

AD 981 Erik the Red discovers Greenland.

AD 1016 Danish King Canute rules England for nearly twenty years, until his death in 1035.

AD 1055 The Viking City of Oslo in Norway is established.

TIME HUNTERS TIMELINE

Tom and Isis never know where in history they'll go to next!
Check out in what order their adventures *actually* happen.

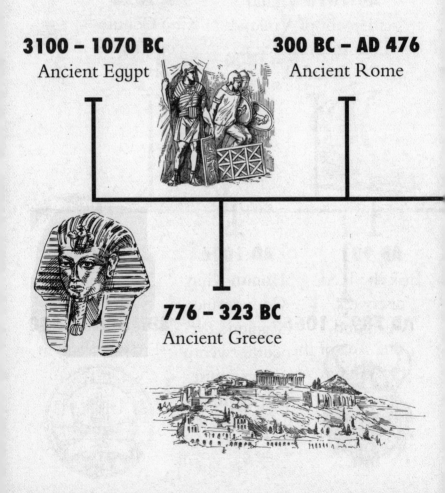

3100 – 1070 BC
Ancient Egypt

300 BC – AD 476
Ancient Rome

776 – 323 BC
Ancient Greece

AD 1000 – 1300
The Middle Ages

AD 789 – 1066
The Age of the
Vikings

AD 1500 – 1830
Era of piracy in
the Caribbean

FANTASTIC FACTS

Impress your friends with these facts about Vikings.

➤ Vikings had an interesting use for skulls. They would wash them out, fill  the eyes, nose and ear holes with wax and use them to drink from.
Now that's a deadly cocktail!

➤ The word 'berserk' comes from the Berserkers, who were vicious Viking warriors. They were so tough that they wore animal skins instead of armour, fought in a 'trance-like' state and had terrifying battle cries.
Yikes!

In Viking times children would become adults when they turned twelve.
No more homework – woohoo!

 Greenland was named 'green' by Erik the Red to trick people into settling there. It was actually very icy and cold.
Brrrr!

 Viking men were often given nicknames based on their appearance or personality, like Eric Bloodaxe, King Sven Forkbeard and Harald Bluetooth Gormsson.
What would your Viking name be?

WHO IS THE MIGHTIEST?

Collect the Gaming Cards and play!

Battle with a friend to find out which historical hero is the mightiest of them all!

Players: 2
Number of Cards: 4+ each

 Players start with an equal number of cards. Decide which player goes first.

 Player 1: choose a category from your first card (Brain Power, Fear Factor, Bravery or Weapon), and read out the score.

 Player 2: read out the stat from the same category on your first card.

➤ The player with the highest score wins the round, takes their opponent's card and puts it at the back of their own pack.

➤ The winning player then chooses a category from the next card and play continues.

➤ The game continues until one player has won all the cards. The last card played wins the title 'Mightiest hero of them all!'

VIKINGS

ERIK the RED

Brain Power	
Fear Factor	305
Bravery	235
Weapon: Axe	260
	310
TOTAL	**1110**

For more fantastic games go to:
www.time-hunters.com

BATTLE THE MIGTHTIEST!

Collect a new set of mighty warriors — free in every
Time Hunters book! Have you got them all?

GLADIATORS

- [ ] Hilarus
- [ ] Spartacus
- [ ] Flamma
- [ ] Emperor Commodus

KNIGHTS

- [ ] King Arthur
- [ ] Galahad
- [ ] Lancelot
- [ ] Gawain

VIKINGS

- [ ] Erik the Red
- [ ] Harald Bluetooth
- [ ] Ivar the Boneless
- [ ] Canute the Great

GREEKS

- ☐ Hector
- ☐ Ajax
- ☐ Achilles
- ☐ Odysseus

Coming soon!

PIRATES

- ☐ Blackbeard
- ☐ Captain Kidd
- ☐ Henry Morgan
- ☐ Calico Jack

EGYPTIANS

- ☐ Anubis
- ☐ King Tut
- ☐ Isis
- ☐ Tom

Who were the Spartans?
What were they fighting for?
And why did they need a wooden horse?

Join Tom and Isis on another action-packed
Time Hunters adventure!

"We need clues," Tom said.

He looked around. To his right, as far as
he could see, were pale stone walls reaching
up to the blue sky. To his left, the green sea
was fringed by dazzlingly white sand. The

beach was teaming with—

"Soldiers!" Isis cried.

Tom held his hand over her mouth and dragged her behind a sand dune. "Shhh!" he said. "Not so loud. Let's work out who these guys are before—"

"First of all," Isis scoffed, "it's my job to talk loudly. I'm a princess! Second of all, they might be able to tell us where my amulet is."

Tom squinted at the soldiers' uniforms. On top of bright red tunics they wore bronze breastplates that made them all look as though they had rippling muscles. On their legs, they wore sandals with straps that held metal shin pads in place. They carried round shields with pictures on the front – some showed winged horses and some had the letter V upside down. But best of all...

"See those plumed helmets?" Tom said.

"I've seen those in Dad's museum. They're Ancient Greek army helmets. And that upside-down V was the symbol of the Spartan army." He peered up at the pale stone walls. "Those look like the walls to some ancient city. But the Greeks are on the outside, so—"

"They've got lovely horses," Isis said. She climbed on to Tom's back for a better look. "Stallions!" she said. "And they're tied together in groups. I think these soldiers are getting ready for battle."

Tom nodded. He looked up at a tall wooden contraption that loomed high above the soldiers. It looked like a giant catapult made from enormous planks of wood, levers and ropes.

"What's that ugly thing?" Isis asked.

Tom racked his brains for the name. He

had seen a diagram of one in his history books. "It's a trebuchet!" he said, suddenly remembering. "They plonk massive boulders into the hammock thingy on the end of the rope and catapult them against the city walls."

"The Greeks are planning an invasion," Isis said, stroking Cleo as she scanned the beach. "So it's going to be chaos at any moment. We'd better find out where to look for Anubis's amulet, quick!"

THE HUNT CONTINUES...

Travel through time with Tom and Isis as they battle the
mightiest warriors of the past. Will they find all six amulets,
or will Isis be banished from the Afterlife forever?

Find out in:

Got it!

☐

Got it!

☐

Got it!

☐

Tick off the books as you collect them!

Go to:

www.time-hunters.com

Travel through time and join the hunt for the
mightiest heroes and villains of history to win
brilliant prizes!

For more adventures, awesome card
games, competitions and thrilling news,
scan this QR code*: